Three Winter Tales

Three Winter Tales

Aisha Bushby

Gaby Verdooren

Collins

Contents

Meet Bea the whiskered bat............ 2

Bea's world 4

Chapter 1 7

Chapter 2 19

Meet Freddy the common frog......... 30

Freddy's world................... 32

Chapter 3 35

Chapter 4 47

Meet Holly the hedgehog 56

Holly's world 58

Chapter 5 61

Chapter 6 73

How can we help animals in the winter? . . 82

What affects hibernation? 84

About the author. 86

About the illustrator 88

Book chat 90

Meet Bea the whiskered bat

Bea is a whiskered bat, a small and furry bat species found in the UK. She's just four centimetres in height which means she could fit into your school pencil case with room for your colouring pencils AND eraser! But her favourite place to roost (which is the name for where she lives) is in a tree, or sometimes on the roof of an old house.

Bea roosts with her family, called a colony. Sometimes there are up to 50 bats in a colony. Bea hunts for moths and flying insects at night and sleeps during the day. You might even spot her in your garden! She learnt to fly when she was three weeks old, and when she was six weeks old, she learnt to hunt for herself, too.

As the weather starts to get colder in the autumn, Bea and her colony will become less active until they enter full hibernation. This means they will sleep for the rest of winter, until the frost melts and flowers bloom in spring. But what would happen if Bea and her colony couldn't find a safe place to hibernate?

Bea's world

village houses

woodlands

field

park

trees

road

trees

leaf pile

allotment

compost heap

bonfire

field

pond

wetlands

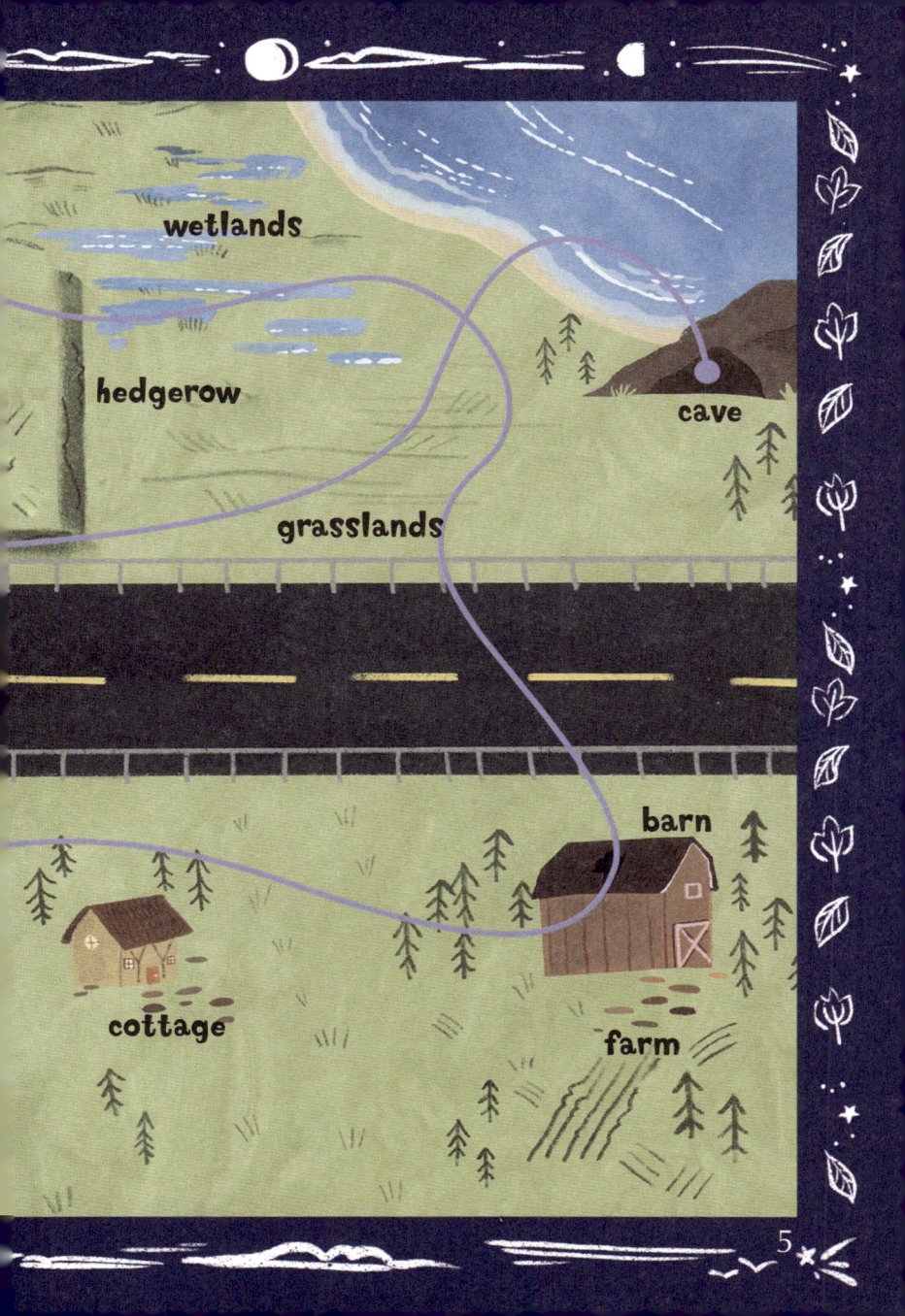

hedgerow

grasslands

cave

barn

cottage

farm

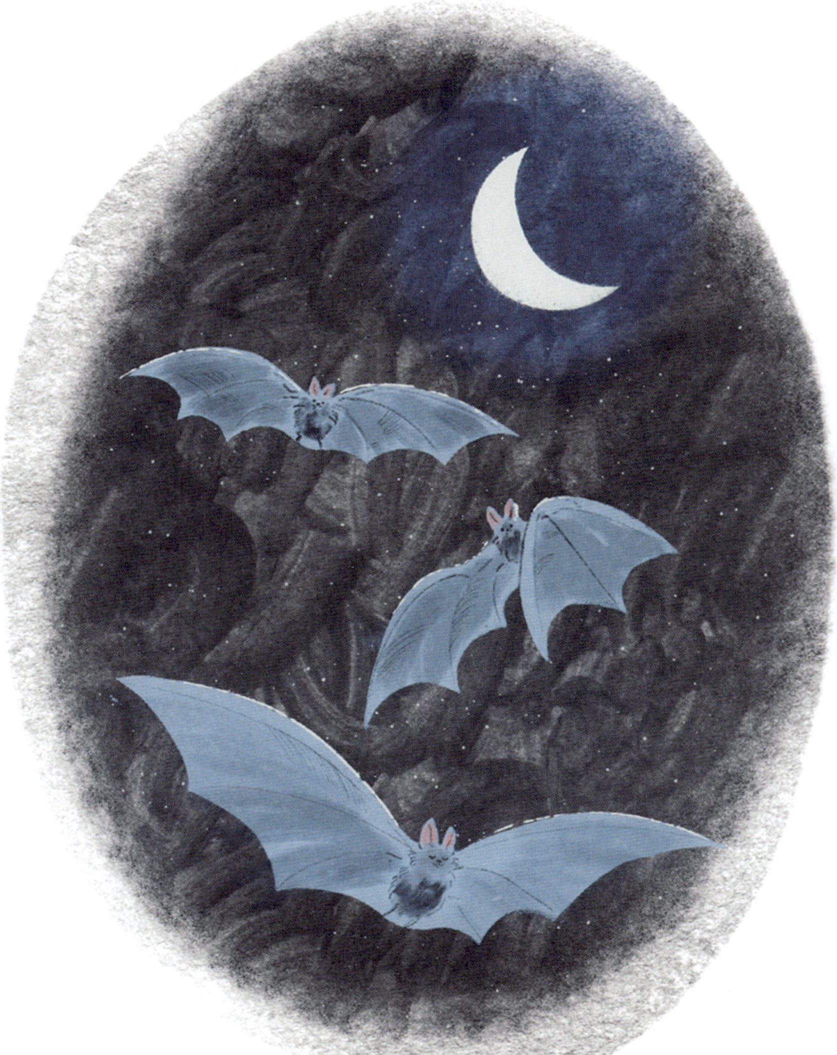

Chapter 1

I unwrap my wings from around my body and peer at the world upside-down from where I'm hanging. The full moon is out and the sky is purple and blue, as nighttime approaches.

It's close to the end of October, and the weather is turning colder. But it's still warmer than it was the year before, and the year before that, according to the other bats in my colony. I don't know much about the previous winters myself because I was only born in July, but I'm learning quickly. I'm three months old now and this is my first winter. I'm excited to get ready for my first hibernation, which is what I'll be doing tonight!

It's been a noisy day in the village where I live, with lots of tractors and vans driving around making noises. Because my hearing is really good, the sounds woke me up during the day, even though I'd usually sleep for around 20 hours. I'm a little tired, but I still get up to start the two very important jobs I have ahead of me, and I hope I'll have enough energy for them both.

My first job is to build up my fat stores to make sure I have enough food to last me through the long winter. That sounds fun to me, because who doesn't enjoy eating their favourite snacks? My second job is a little more difficult. I need to find a safe place for me and my colony to hibernate this winter.

We need somewhere humans won't disturb us, but also somewhere that will stay warm and humid. It's a tough job in such a busy village, but I'm up for the challenge! I hope I make them proud …

I fly across the village and make sure I stay away from the dots of light coming from the windows of the houses below. The bright lights that humans use in their homes are a little annoying, but I've got used to them now.

Once I accidentally flew into the window of a house. It was terrifying! The humans in the room jumped up and ran away like *I* was the scary one. But *they* were scarier, waving their arms and screaming! The noises they made were so loud it confused me, making it difficult for me to find the open window again. Eventually I escaped, after one human opened the window wide. I've never, ever gone near a house again.

I also make sure I stay away from chimneys which have smoke puffing out of them, because that can be quite dangerous for bats like me. I don't go near any humans when they're outside, either. This is because any noises they make can confuse me while I'm trying to hunt. And tonight, I need to work extra hard to make sure I eat enough food to last me the winter!

Once I'm safely away from humans and out in the open where lots of insects are roaming, I let out a stream of high-pitched sounds. I know whenever there's an insect around because the sound I make bounces off them and comes back to me. It's so exciting when I realise I've found something! That's when I swoop and dive. I can catch insects mid-flight and keep going without stopping at all. I'm really fast too, so the insects never know I'm coming.

Other times, with bigger catches, I'll stop and hang upside-down again, giving myself time to eat.

Tonight, I manage to gather a few midges and moths, as well as the odd spider, but I'm struggling to find enough food to keep me full over the winter, which makes me a little worried. Many of the insects I'd like to hunt live inside human homes, and I *definitely* don't want to go in one of those again. Moths build cocoons in dusty attics, and spiders spin their webs near the ceilings. It's quite clever of them to do that, but it means I'll have to leave the village and find somewhere wild to hunt.

I have two options tonight: the woodlands to the left of the village, or the wetlands to the right. I'm happy to travel a few kilometres every night to find my food, and so I decide to visit both.

First, I turn left towards the woodlands, where I fly beneath the canopy of the trees. I notice that there are plenty of hollow trees where my colony and I might be able to hibernate, and I'm excited to tell them about it.

Here, I find plenty of insects, including hundreds and thousands of ants. It takes me just one hour to eat one thousand ants!

Satisfied, I make my way to the wetlands to get a little more food to last me the winter.

I fly through the village and towards the wetlands so quickly that I'm just a blur in the sky.

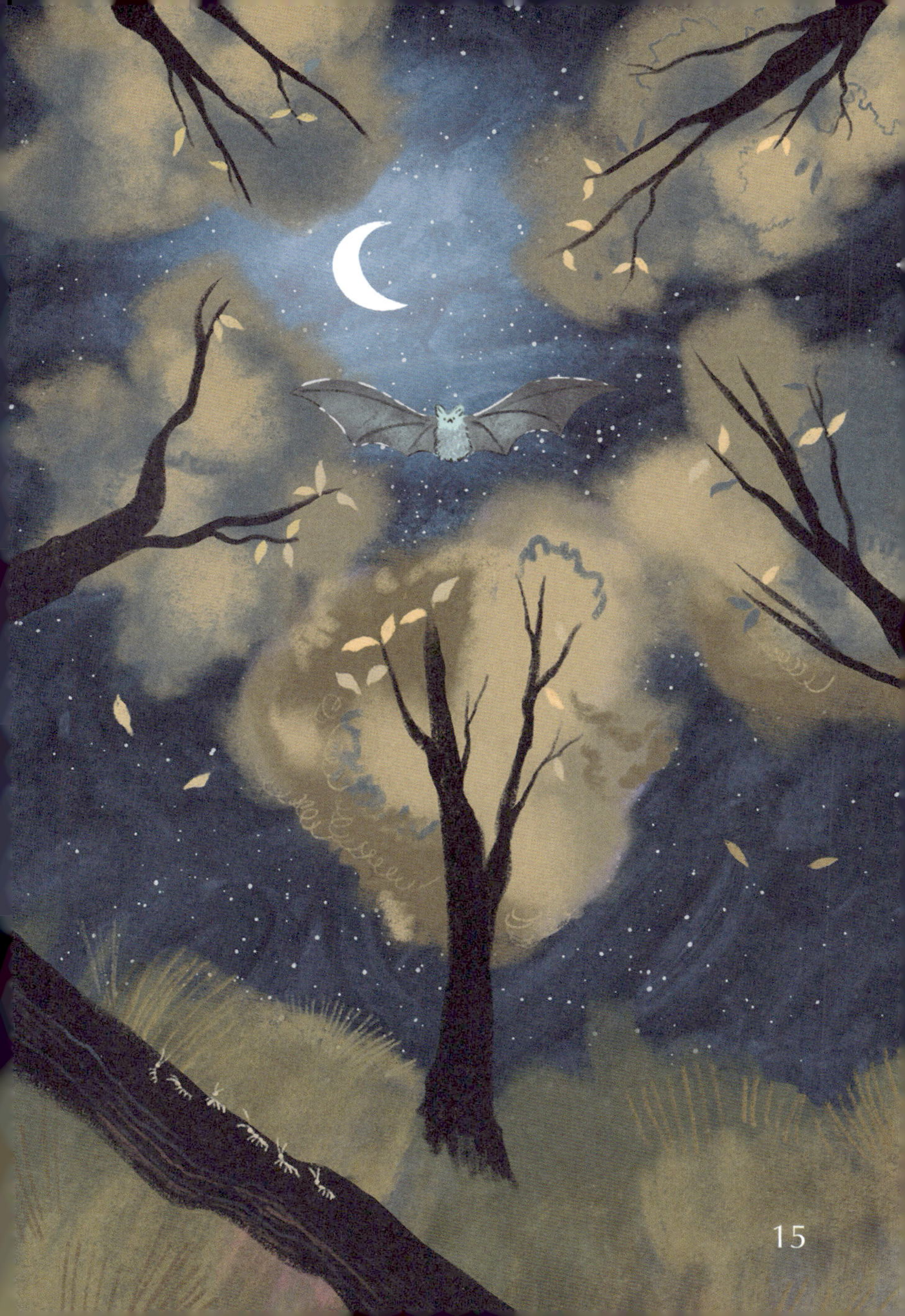

At the wetlands, I dip down close to the surface of the water where lots of different species of bird live and eat together. That means there'll be enough food for me too, because if there wasn't, then the birds would have found somewhere else to live.

At the edge of the water is tall grass, about the height of a table. Beyond that, I notice a cave near the sea which is another place my colony could hibernate. I'm pleased to have found two good options for us! In the tall grass are hundreds and thousands of mosquitoes. I eat as many as I can in the time I have left and make my way back home to start the next part of my mission: finding a safe place to hibernate.

17

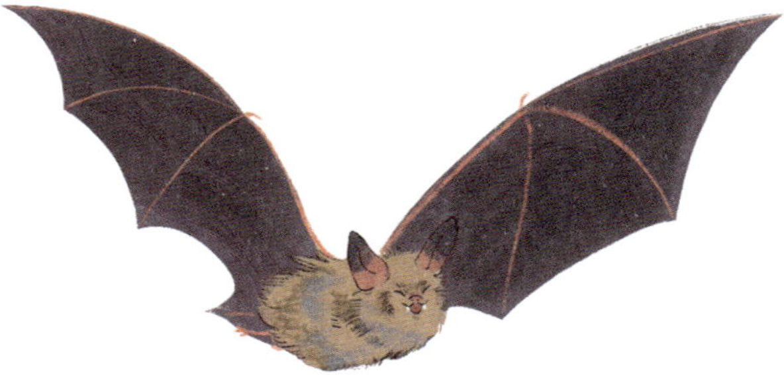

Chapter 2

I fly back to my roost to tell my colony about the two locations I've found for us to hibernate: the woodlands and the wetlands. On the way back to the roost, I find an abandoned barn at the edge of a farm. It's large, with plenty of room and away from humans. I decide to inspect it a little more closely to see if I can add it to my list of options.

I land on a wooden rafter, and notice it goes all of the way across the barn leaving enough room for all of us to hibernate together. But then I spot some things that make me feel a little worried.

There are planks of wood and bundles of hay everywhere, and there's even a broken tractor.

Though there aren't any humans here right now, they might come in during the winter to use the hay to feed their farm animals. Or they might try to fix the broken tractor.

I also notice that half of the roof is missing which means the temperature might fluctuate from warm to cold. Plus, because the farmers look after their crops carefully, there aren't many insects around for us to eat during the winter in case we wake up and need more food. I see enough to know that the barn isn't a good option for me and my colony. Even though I'm disappointed, I still have two good options. I head back to my colony to let them know about the woodlands and wetlands, and I hope one of them will be just the right place.

They're pleased with what I've discovered. I'm proud of myself, but tired too, and I'll soon need another 20 hours of sleep. I promise my colony I'll return to the woodlands and wetlands the next evening to check the two options again. It's lucky I found the woodlands and wetlands today, because the night has turned cold and it looks like it's time for us to hibernate!

The village is much quieter the next day. I get more sleep and wake up feeling well-rested. I'm excited to visit the woodlands and wetlands again tonight, and fly straight to the woodlands as soon as I'm awake.

I shoot through the sky like a star, watching as the humans turn their lights on one by one far below. I fly high above the houses and get there quickly. It's colder than it was the day before, with frost covering the grass and leaves. I'm not used to feeling this cold and I'm looking forward to finding somewhere cosy to hibernate soon.

Back in the woodlands, I hunt again, more quickly this time, because I know the best spots to find food. Then, I inspect the tree hollows. They offer lots of protection and are just big enough for me and some of my colony to fit inside.

They're nice and damp inside, which means there'll be plenty of insects, and the temperature shouldn't fluctuate from warm to cold like the barn. But the problem is that we'd need a few tree hollows to fit us all in and, although there are thousands of trees in the forest, not all of them have hollows. It'll take me all night to search!

As I go to leave, feeling more and more like the woodlands might not be the best option, I hear a piercing sound that terrifies me … a barking dog!

I make sure I stay well away but I find a human crunching along the ground just behind the dog, which is roaming free.

The dog sniffs around and stops just next to the tree I'm in. It looks up, as if it notices me, and lets out another ear-piercing bark.

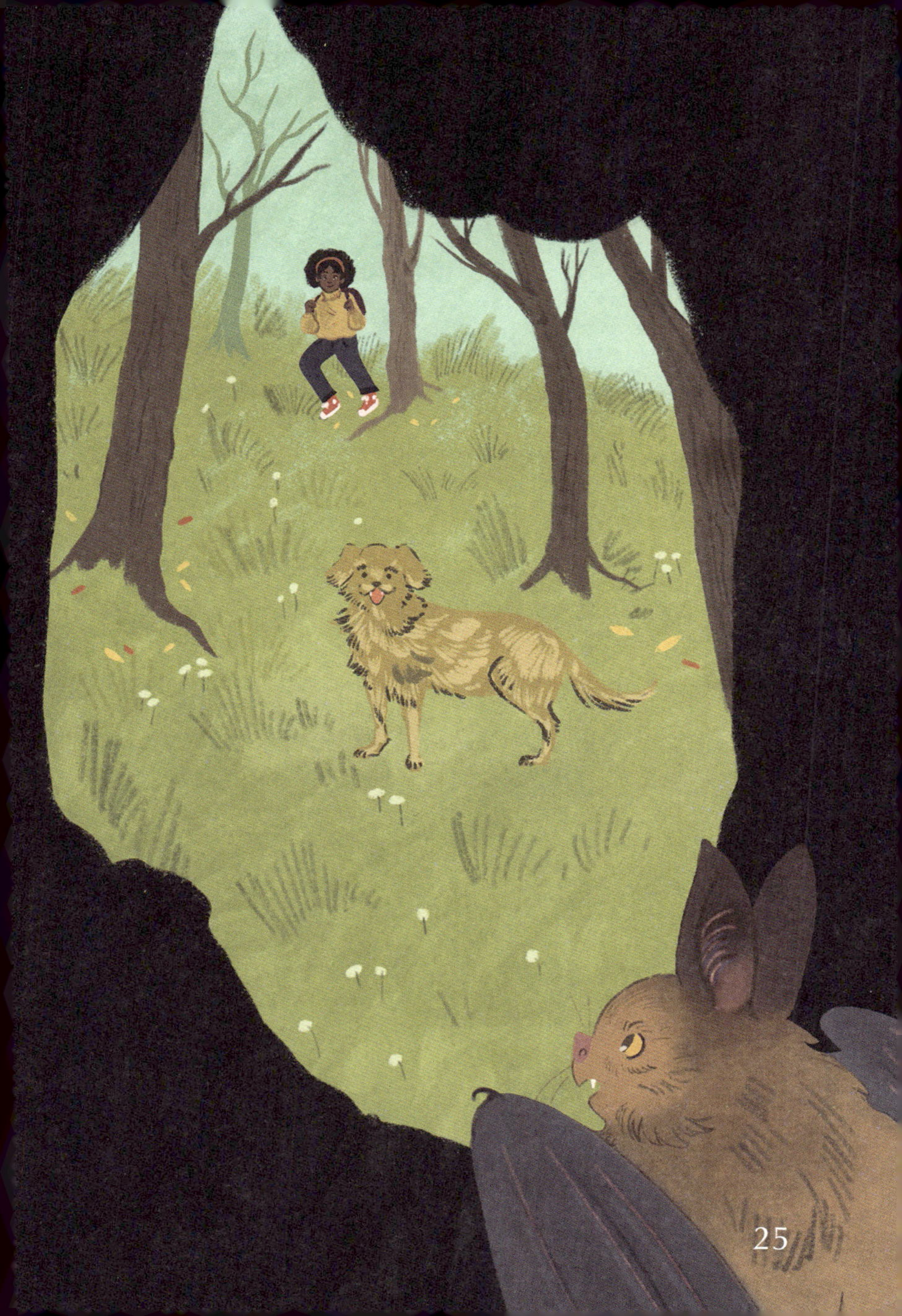

I fly away quickly, and head towards the wetlands far away from the dog and human. It's too risky to bring my colony here, so I don't try to search for any other tree hollows.

As I head towards the wetlands, I start to feel a little dejected. Because humans take up so much space, it makes it difficult to find somewhere safe and quiet to hibernate where we can have plenty of food within our reach. With our last option ahead of me, I hope the cave in the wetlands ends up being a safe place to hibernate!

As I get closer to the cave, I spot something that makes me feel hopeful again. You can't get to the cave on foot because it's facing the sea, which means there's no way humans (or dogs) could come inside it during the winter. Once inside, I notice something else that makes me feel even more hopeful. The cave is damp and cool. And because it's enclosed, it means the temperature will probably stay constant. Best of all, the cave is *huge*. There's more than enough room for me and all my colony to fit in together. Plus, given all of the insects I found yesterday, I know there's lots of food nearby.

My worry turns to excitement as I realise I've done it: I've found a safe, quiet place for me and my colony to hibernate! I head straight back to them and wait for everyone to return from their night's hunt.

When they return, I tell them about my search and how I've found a perfect spot for us all. Then, before the sun rises again and the humans wake to start their day, we all fly to the wetlands. I feel a bit nervous – I hope everyone will like the cave I've found! But I needn't have worried. Soon enough, we're all settled down in the lovely, roomy cave for a long and peaceful sleep!

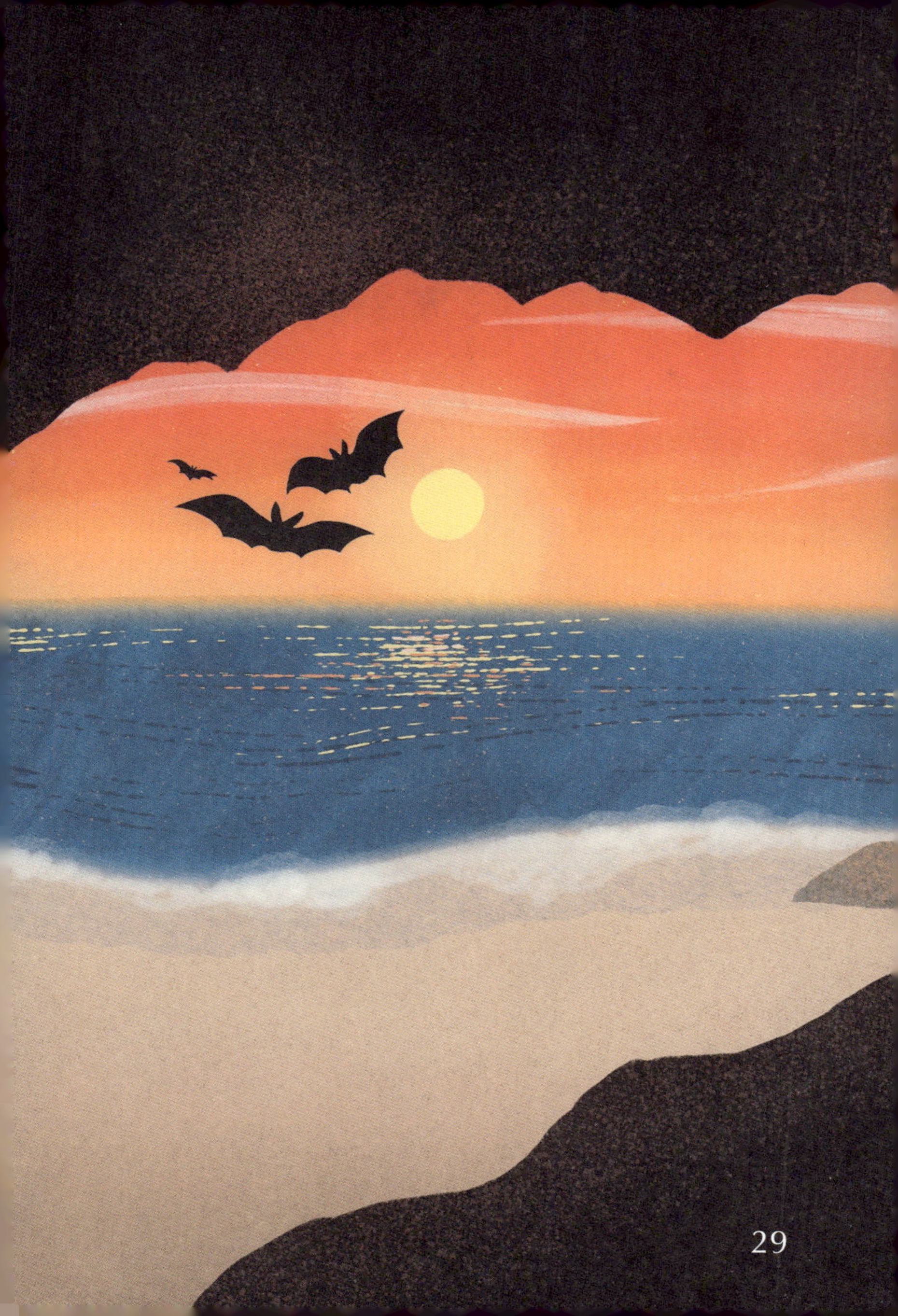

Meet Freddy the common frog

Freddy is a common frog, and is a similar size to a classroom stapler. There are only two species of frog found in the UK and two species of toad. The main difference between frogs and toads is that toads have bumpy, rough skin, while frogs have smooth skin.

Frogs like to live in woodlands, gardens, hedgerows and grasslands. They live together in groups called an army and sometimes travel as far as five kilometres from their home.

Freddy started his life as a tadpole, when his mother laid her eggs in a pond. Tadpoles live fully underwater until they develop back legs and front legs and turn into froglets (the name for a baby frog).

Freddy, like all frogs, can't control his body temperature the way humans can, which means that when the winter comes, he needs to stay somewhere warm to hibernate. Frogs also need to make sure their skin stays moist, and so they need to live somewhere where they won't dry out. They like hibernating underground, or inside compost heaps – as long as they don't get disturbed!

Freddy's world

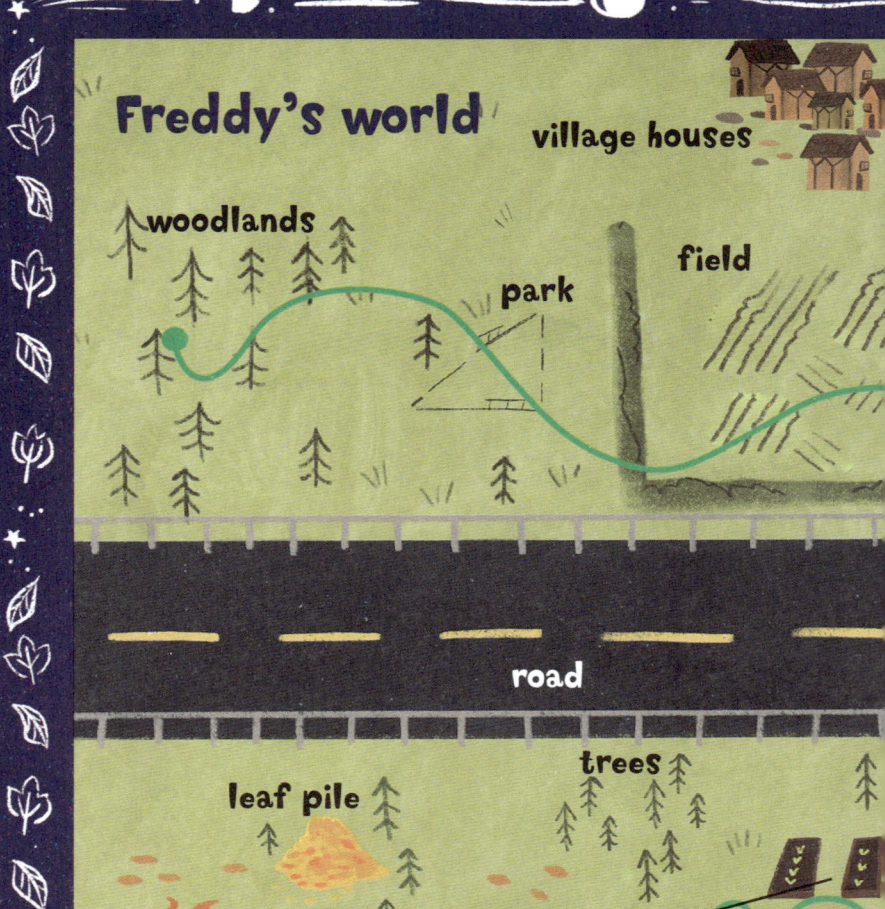

village houses

woodlands

park

field

road

trees

leaf pile

allotment

bonfire

field

compost heap

pond

wetlands

hedgerow

cave

grasslands

cottage

farm

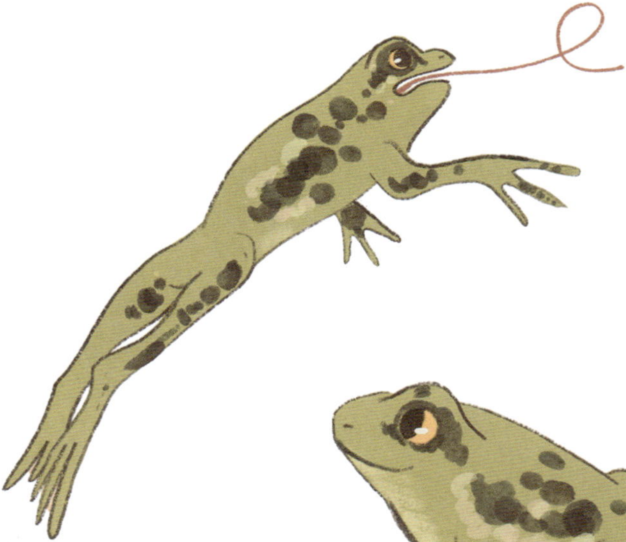

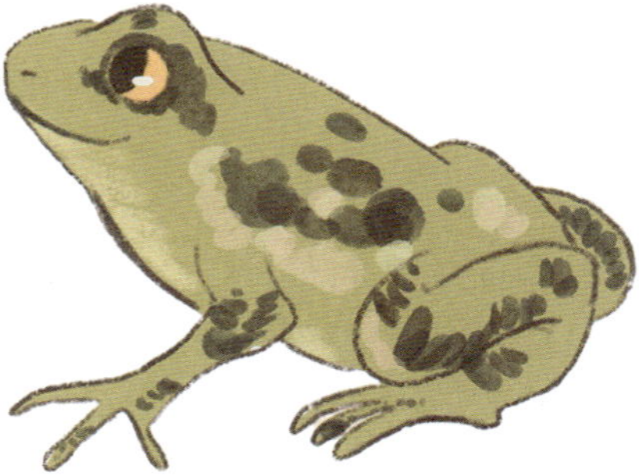

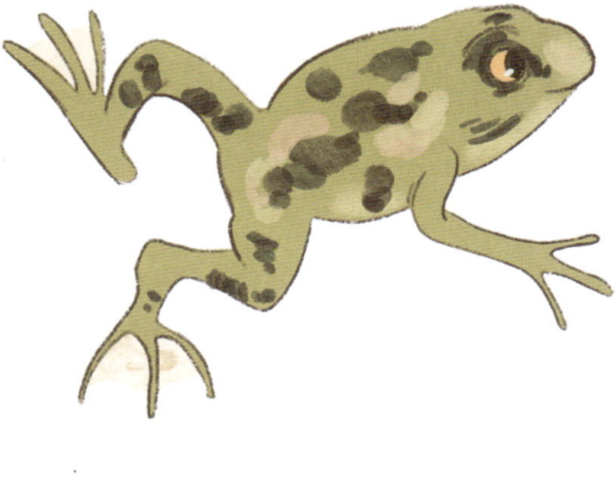

Chapter 3

I wake up from a deep sleep to find the weather is mild today, even though it's the middle of winter. I'm glad because it means I can get up and search for some food. I only need to eat every month or so, while I'm hibernating. Because my body is moving more slowly, I need less food to sustain me. Still, I feel pretty hungry, and I'm looking forward to enjoying a nice evening snack.

Mostly, I like to eat moths and other insects. But I also like snails, slugs and worms. You should watch me eat a snail – I can gobble it up whole, using my long tongue and sticky saliva. I bet *you* can't do that!

Luckily for me, there are plenty of worms, slugs and snails in the compost heap I've been sleeping in for the winter, so I take my time and eat all the ones I can find. I'm still hungry when I've finished eating, so I decide to stretch my legs and search for more food in the garden.

The moon is high, the sky is dotted with stars, and the air is damp – just how I like it. I crawl out of the compost heap in a good mood, landing on the ground with a thud. I'm living in a human's garden, and I can see vegetable patches in front of me which are ready to plant in the spring. There are dead flowers, too, but their plants are waiting to bloom again once the temperature grows warmer.

I'm excited for spring! My plan is to find a nice big pond where I'll let out my loudest croak to find a mate. I've practised lots and, before we all started hibernating, all of my friends agreed I had the loudest croak of them all. I wonder what they're all doing now and whether they're in a deep sleep, or searching for food like me. I hope they're safe, and that I can see them again when the weather is warmer.

But for now, I need to stay silent, because there might be predators waiting for me. I wouldn't want to attract a heron's attention, for example. It might swoop down from the sky and eat me!

I also need to stay well out of the sight of foxes, who are often hungrier in the winter because there are lots of hibernating animals. Even cats are a source of danger.

Though they get food at home from their humans, and frogs aren't really the sort of animals they like to eat, they still try to hunt us whenever they can.

As I'm searching for some more worms, slugs and snails in the vegetable patches, two shining yellow eyes appear in the distance. I freeze, watching the eyes blink very slowly, while I figure out how I might escape. Because I can tell, whatever it is that's watching me, is out to hunt.

The creature moves quickly on soft paw pads and leaps, landing in front of me. I see two triangular ears and a long bushy tail, which means it could be a cat or fox. But as soon as I hear the chirping noise it makes, I can tell it's the cat that lives in the house. It has long grey and white fur and its mouth is open wide, ready to gobble me up the way I'd gobbled the snails. It hadn't noticed me when I was in the compost heap before, but it does now.

41

For a moment, my whole life flashes before my eyes. I remember being born in a lovely pond as a tadpole, stepping on land for the first time, and hibernating for the first time this winter. I don't want to miss seeing my first spring season after I've worked so hard to stay alive. I shake off my fear and move quickly. First, I let out a great big scream that startles the cat. And then I leap high into the air, landing about a metre away from it.

It takes the cat a minute to figure out what I've done, and where I've gone, which gives me the chance to escape. To my left is the compost heap I've been hibernating in. It's familiar to me, and it's been safe, so far. I don't know if this is the right choice, but I decide to jump back inside it, hoping the cat doesn't notice. But it does!

As I bury myself deeper into the compost heap, the cat digs quickly behind me, flinging vegetable peelings and grass cuttings everywhere. I feel its hot breath on my back, and I know its sharp claws are just centimetres away from scratching me.

I manage to slip out through a small gap in the side of the compost heap back into the open garden. The cat is so distracted by its digging that it doesn't notice me at first. *Finally*, something is going my way! I look around, trying to find somewhere to escape to. That's when I spot it: a glistening pond. It's not as big as the pond I'd like to visit in the spring, but it'll do for now.

I leap towards the pond, and the cat notices me when I'm about halfway there. Cats are fast, so it catches up quickly, leaping through the air with its paws outstretched. It's so close I can feel its whiskers brush the back of my legs. But I land in the pond with a big splash that scares the cat away. It runs all the way back indoors. I even find some snails at the bottom of the pond to gobble up. I'm safe and well-fed, ready for another long sleep as the winter turns cold again.

45

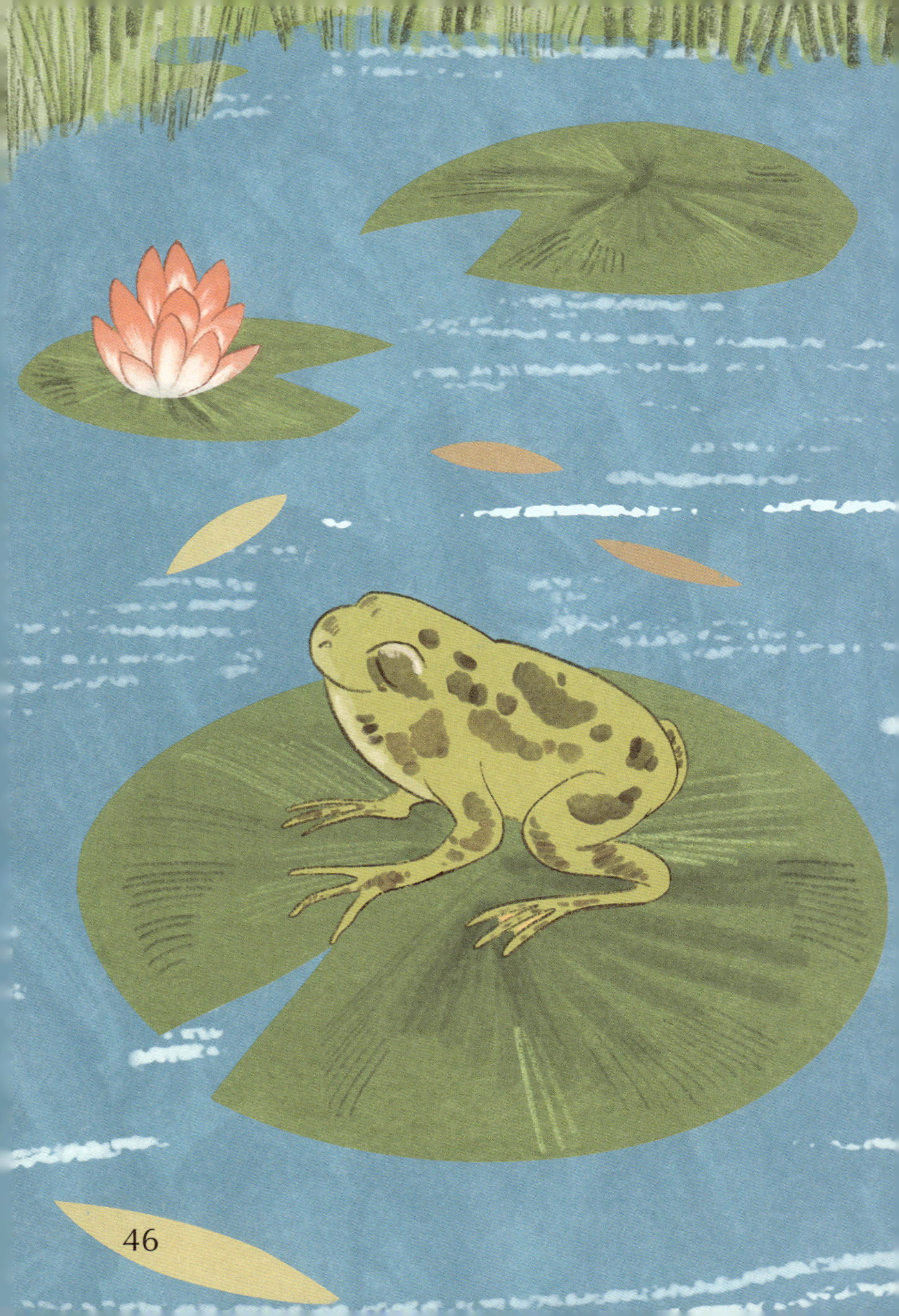

Chapter 4

I managed to gather enough food – before the cat tried to attack me – to stay full for another month. This is good, because it means I don't have to worry about being hunted by the cat again, as it won't want to stick its paws in the bottom of the pond where I'm sleeping. But I need to be careful as the weather turns colder.

Small garden ponds can freeze if the temperature drops too much, and I need to stay warm, or else I'll die! I need to find somewhere else to sleep – without any other predators around to catch me.

When I step out of the pond again (this time making sure the cat is nowhere to be found), I check the compost heap I was in before. I notice there's some equipment next to it this time, which means the humans have been using it. I don't want to be disturbed by humans, and I definitely don't want to run into the cat again. I think it's time to leave the garden and find somewhere else to hibernate for when the temperature gets even colder.

Nearby are woodlands, grassland and hedgerows. The hedgerow is just across the road by a field. To the right of the field is the grassland, by the marsh. And to the left of the field are the woodlands. I can't travel too far, so I need to consider my options carefully.

Because the hedgerow is just across the road, I decide to start there. But first, I have to cross a busy road …

There are cars coming from both directions, and sometimes tractors, too. They move much too quickly for me to be able to cross fast enough to avoid them, and so I wait for some time until there's a big gap. As I'm making my way towards the fields with the hedgerows, I notice the ground has started to vibrate a little which makes the gravel bounce around like crickets.

I look up to see a car fast approaching like a hungry monster. Somehow, it's much scarier than the cat was! I need to move, but it's so quick that it drives straight over me.

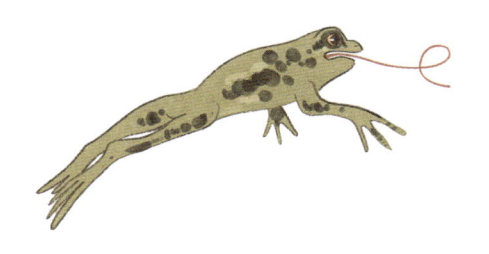

For a moment I freeze, thinking I've been run over. Then I see two tyre marks on either side of me – I realise that the car has gone over me but the wheels haven't hit me. How lucky! But I can't stay out here for long, because more cars are approaching in the distance. With the last of my strength, I make it the rest of the way across safely.

Once I'm at the hedgerow, I notice there are plenty of insects for me to nibble on, and the branches of the hedge will shelter me from predators. But the ground beneath the soil is thick with roots. This means there isn't anywhere for me to dig and burrow inside, so I can't hibernate here. I decide to visit this hedgerow again in the spring, as I bet there will be plenty more insects to eat around then. I won't need to bury myself in the soil in the spring as I'll be spending most of my time in the water.

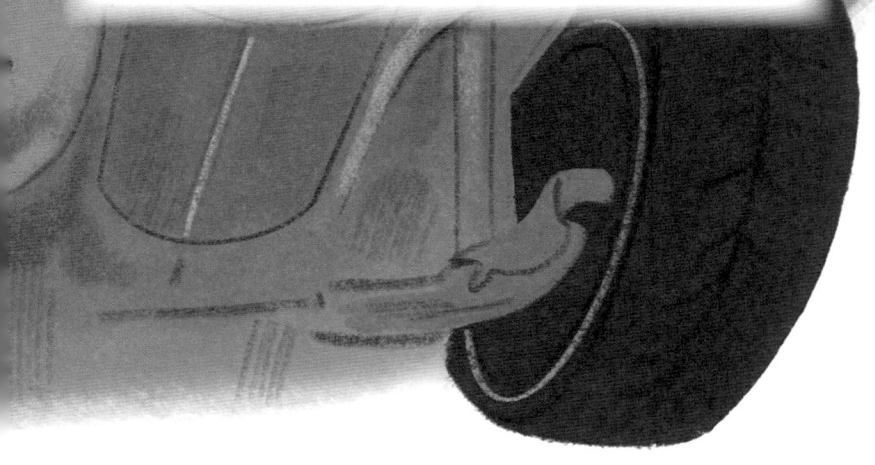

For now, I need somewhere damp and warm enough to stay asleep for a long time. I also need somewhere I won't be disturbed again!

I take some time to rest as I look left towards the woods and right towards the grasslands. That's where I spot them, coming from the nature reserve. A great big flock of birds fly into the sky, which makes me think there must be dangerous predators like herons. Perhaps it's best to stay away from the grasslands, for now. I'll try the woodlands instead.

The sun is beginning to set as I approach a park where children are playing with their parents nearby. They're gathering their coats and bags as they get ready to go home for the night.

There are dogs which sniff the ground, their noses coming dangerously close to me, and some children who spot me and want to pick me up. But human skin can be poisonous to us frogs because of the soaps and oils they use. Luckily, one of the parents tells their children not to touch me, and they wave goodbye instead.

It takes me almost five kilometres of travelling to get to the woodlands, which is as far as I can go in one night. I get there just as the sun begins to rise. I was lucky not to come across any foxes on my way, and for that, I'm thankful. Still, there will be foxes in the forest, so I need to be extra alert as I search for a place to burrow. Luckily for me, foxes are nocturnal, which means they mainly hunt during the night and sleep during the day. Because it's morning now, that gives me the chance to search for a burrow, and hide before foxes come around again.

The woodlands are quiet. In the distance, I can hear a human's crunching footsteps and a dog's bark, but they sound far away. Nearby, I can hear the odd bird chirping in the trees, but no herons or other dangerous birds of prey are able to reach me because of the cover of the branches overhead.

It doesn't take me long to spot an empty burrow which might have once belonged to a hare or badger. After a very eventful winter, this burrow looks like the perfect place and I'm looking forward to a nice long sleep. I settle down, knowing that soon spring will arrive, and I'll be out and about for more adventures.

Meet Holly the hedgehog

Holly is one of the 200,000 hedgehogs living in gardens and green spaces in the UK. She's about the size of an orange and has long spines (over 5,000!) which she uses to protect herself from predators.

Mainly, she has to be careful around tawny owls and badgers, who love to eat hedgehogs like her. Whenever she feels threatened, she'll curl herself up into a ball and push out her spikes.

Hedgehogs got their name because they like to forage in hedges to find food to eat. Usually they eat insects, worms, and centipedes, but sometimes they can even eat snakes and frogs! This means Holly and Freddy wouldn't get along very well, if they ever met ...

Holly left home when she was six weeks old to look after herself – the same age as Bea when she learnt to fly.

Like Bea and Freddy, Holly will spend the winter hibernating, usually from October to March, depending on how cold it is. In order to prepare for hibernation, hedgehogs collect grass, straw and leaves to create a nest to sleep in over the winter. But what would happen if Holly picked the wrong spot to hibernate?

Holly's world

village houses

woodlands

park

field

road

leaf pile

trees

bonfire

field

compost heap

allotment

pond

wetlands

hedgerow

cave

grasslands

cottage

farm

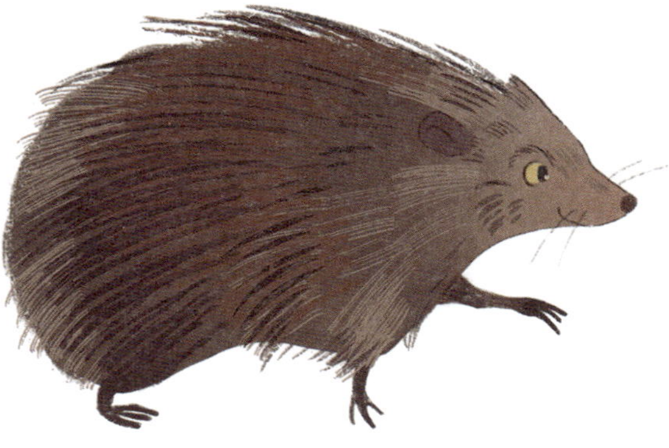

Chapter 5

I'm in a peaceful and very relaxing sleep when I'm woken up by the faint smell of smoke. I can hear crunching footsteps nearby and loud human voices. Immediately, my whole body stiffens as I try to work out what's going on.

It's the beginning of November and I'd just started hibernating for the winter a few days ago. I shouldn't be awake right now, really, as I've had enough food to keep me going through a long winter sleep. Which means something must be wrong. Very wrong. I just wish I understood what.

A few days ago, I found a huge pile of twigs and grass and straw in the middle of a field at the centre of the village. It looked like the perfect place to hibernate because it was warm and cosy. But now I'm not so sure, because there are so many strange and scary smells and noises.

The smell of smoke is growing thicker now, working its way down my throat, making me cough. I can see fire on one side of the nest I'd been resting in. It makes the twigs and straw and grass crackle loudly. Each time it makes a *SNAP* sound, my body shivers with fear. And then I realise, with terror, that the fire is heading in my direction!

63

I need to leave my nest quickly because it's not safe here any more. The only problem is, there are lots of humans all round my nest with big stomping boots. But I need to escape the fire *now*, which means I have no choice but to head in their direction (even though I'd usually stay far away from humans). So, deciding that I have a better chance at avoiding stomping boots than a roaring fire, I crawl out of my nest, the twigs snagging on my pointy spikes.

Once I step out of my nest, the air is cool, and I let out a few more coughs to clear my throat of smoke, hoping it hasn't made me ill. I need to find another nest so I can continue hibernating again soon. But first of all, I need to make it through the crowd of humans.

It's the scariest thing I've ever had to do (besides escaping that burning hot fire), but I have no choice. My survival instincts kick in, telling me I need to be brave to make it through the night.

The humans stand tall, and I'm barely as high as their shoes! They're all facing the nest I was in and staring at the fire that has taken over it. I wonder whether they plan to do something to stop it, but no one's moving. Just watching. And they don't seem as alarmed by it as I am. How strange humans are!

Oh, this is all such a mess! With the heat of the fire behind me, and the cold of the winter in front, I get all muddled and confused. I only have about half an hour until the cold takes over my body and I fall into hibernation again. And I need to make sure I have enough energy to make it to another hibernation nest before that happens. The problem is, I'm not sure I can get through the humans on my own – it's too dangerous. But if I wait for them to leave that could take hours. How will I make sure I survive the night?

It's when I'm desperately trying to figure out what to do that I see a human bend down beneath the barrier and walk towards me. At first, I think they're going to stomp on me with their shoes and I'm so frightened that my instinct is to bite them. But even though my teeth are pointed, they're tiny, only good for nibbling at my food. So, instead, I curl up into a ball and let my spikes protect me.

I sit like that for a long while, wondering if I'm about to be crushed. But nothing happens. I hear human voices speaking to one another, but I don't understand anything they're saying. I wait, and wait, and wait for what seems like ages before I peek up at them. They're chatting and pointing to me. Then, one of them bends down with their hands outstretched. I let out a hiss, as a warning, then curl up into a ball again.

Suddenly, I feel myself lifted into the cold night air and away from the burning fire. Everything is moving too quickly for me to understand what's happening, but the human voices are fading too. All I can hear is the soothing voice of the human carrying me, and even though I still can't understand what they're saying, their voice is gentle and I start to feel less afraid. I think they might be helping me.

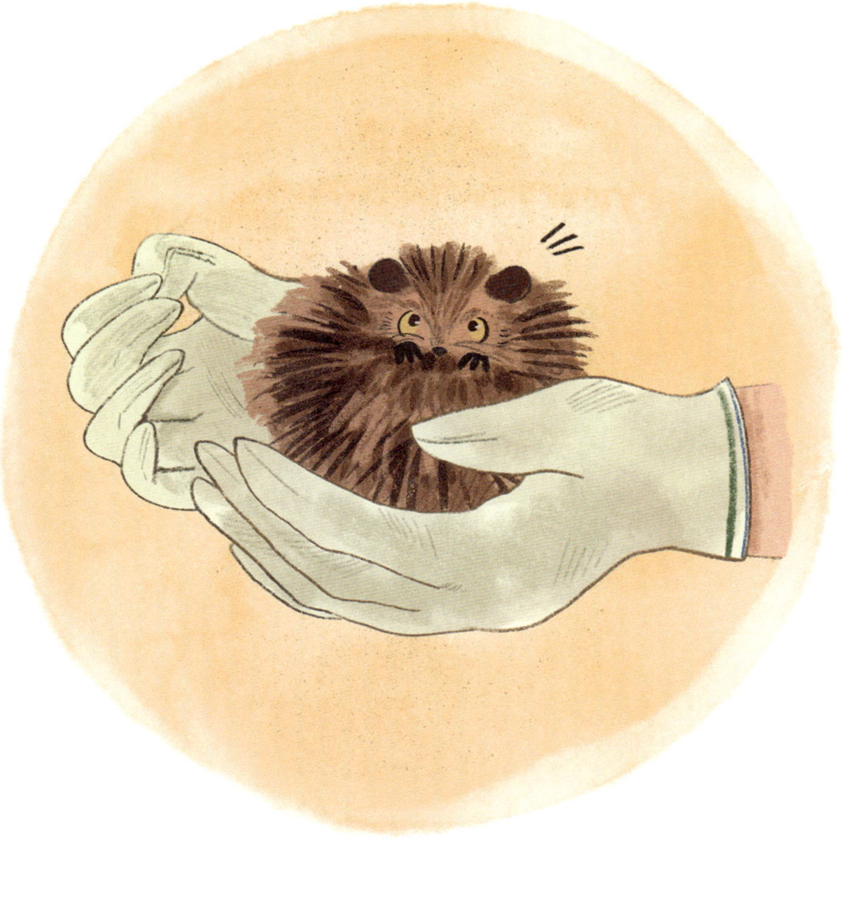

They place me down gently by the edge of the field, by a leaf pile, and I finally decide to unfurl myself so I'm no longer a ball. I peer up at them and watch as they pour something into a bottle lid and place it on the ground next to me. At first, I'm uncertain, and curl up into a ball again to protect myself.

But as they step back to watch me, I realise they've left me some water to drink. I drink it gratefully, because my throat feels itchy from the smoke earlier.

They pour a bit more water, and a bit more after that. Once I stop drinking, they take the lid back and walk away slowly, so as not to startle me. I'm so pleased to be alone and safe by the leaf pile, where I can figure out what I need to do next.

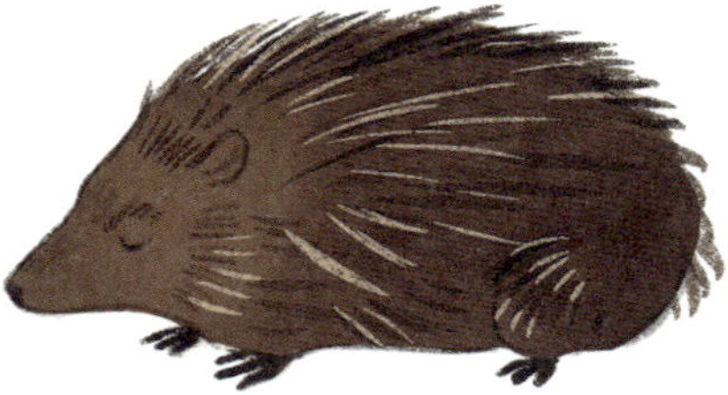

Chapter 6

It takes me some time to recover after my incident with the fire and all the humans, but I feel very lucky to be alive. I've heard lots of tales of hedgehogs who haven't survived the winter. My uncle got caught in a fire once, but he didn't make it out.

It's dark outside, and even though I can see well in the dark, so can all of the predators that might be hunting me. After the scary evening I've had, I'm running low on energy. I need to make sure I eat some more food so I can go back to hibernating.

I also need to find somewhere new to hibernate – somewhere I can build a nest that will be safe from fires, humans, and other dangers that might cross my path.

The leaf pile next to me looks like a cosy spot. Usually, this would be the perfect place to hibernate, but it's a little too close to all the humans still standing in the field. I decide to have a look at the leaf pile anyway, mostly to see if I can forage for some food. I'm finally in luck! I find lots and lots of worms and even a few beetles. When I've eaten enough to gather my energy, I decide to step out of the leaf pile so I can find somewhere else to hibernate.

It was lucky I did that because as I'm leaving, so are the humans! A group of kids run into the leaf pile, throwing leaves everywhere. They startle me and I roll back into a ball until they've gone.

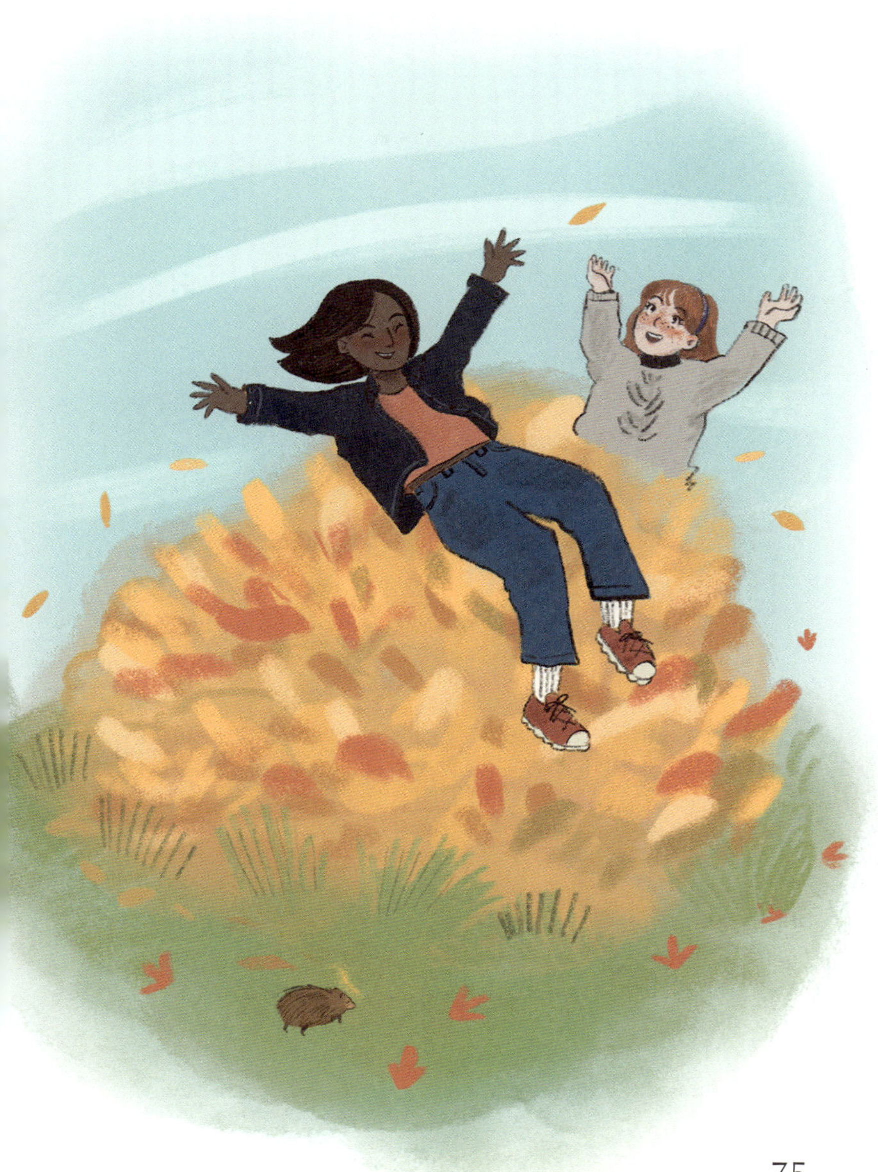

Right next to this field is a house where some humans live. I don't plan on hibernating there, either, because I learnt my lesson the first time. From now on, I plan on hibernating well away from humans. But I *do* know the garden has a cat, and even though it's one of my predators, it also means there is always cat food left in a bowl outside. Plus, cats know to stay away from hedgehog spikes. I'm less afraid of them than I am of foxes, who are wild and hungry.

I'm at the edge of a field, just by a busy road that separates me from another field that has plenty of hedgerow for me to explore. That's where I'd like to go to hibernate, but I can't travel there just yet. The humans are lingering by their cars, chatting. I watch, dazed, as the cars come to life. Their headlights are like two giant eyes, and their engines hum like a cat's growl. If I hadn't heard stories about them before, I'd think they were the scariest predator I'd ever seen.

So, while the humans are busy, I visit the garden. I know my way around well, and head straight for the cat bowl by the front door. Through the window, I can see the cat snoozing in a warm and cosy bed. So long as I keep watching it, I'll be safe. There's a bowl of water too, and I drink some more, then I munch on some cat food and biscuits. It's delicious! I'm so distracted by the food – and making sure the cat is still asleep – that I forget to watch my back. It's only when I hear a nearby owl hoot a warning that I turn to peer into the darkness. There I see it, hiding in the bushes: a fox!

I do what I always do when I'm in danger: I roll into a ball and push my spikes out. A few moments pass and I can feel the presence of the fox nearby, but then I hear a *SLURP* noise, followed by a *SNUFFLE*. I take a little peek and see that the fox isn't interested in me at all! It only wants the cat food, like I do.

The fox's fur looks so matted and worn that I don't even feel annoyed that it's eaten the rest of the food. We lock eyes for a moment, each of us understanding how hard it is to survive in the wild, before the fox walks away. Even though it's one of my predators, I know it prefers the soft and easy cat food. Usually, foxes will only eat a hedgehog that is already dead, and I'm very much alive!

It's time, now, for me to find somewhere new to hibernate. I zigzag my way through the garden, past a pond, some vegetable patches and a compost heap, towards the road. Luckily, it's empty. I cross quickly and safely, feeling excited as I approach my new hibernation spot.

This field is different from the last one. Instead of grass, there are neat rows of soil ready for new seeds to be sown in the spring. And all around the field is a great big hedgerow.

I make sure I travel far enough that I'm well away from any humans. After a bit of searching, I find the perfect spot in the hedgerow to build my nest. By the time I get there, I'm exhausted. Luckily there is plenty of food – including berries – for me to nibble on before I build my nest. Yum!

I eat until I'm full and then use the loose twigs and leaves from the bottom of the hedge to build myself a nest. I do this by snuffling around with my nose close to the mud.
I gather what I need in my mouth, and put it all together in a pile.

As the temperature drops further, I fall fast asleep, knowing this time I'm safe to hibernate until the spring arrives in full bloom.

How can we help animals in the winter?

The best way to help animals to survive the winter is to provide plenty of water and food.

If you have a pond you can pop a ball in to stop the water from completely freezing over.

This means animals can access water, and it keeps the oxygen flowing for any frogs that might be hibernating in the pond.

It's all about being mindful of the creatures that we share the world with and thinking of ways we can avoid disturbing them while we go about our days.

What affects hibernation?

1 Climate change
Climate change has created warmer weather during the winter. Lots of animals that would usually hibernate during the coldest months are waking up too early. This means they use up their fat stores before there is more food available.

2 Predators
Hibernation means that animals are not out in the open where predators can catch them. But hibernation also means that animals are vulnerable, so they need to find somewhere secret to hide where predators won't find them.

3 Humans

Humans can accidentally disturb animals by making too much noise, or building where animals would usually hibernate. It's important for us to be mindful of our surroundings as we move about the world.

About the author

A bit about me …

I was born in the Middle East and now live in the UK. When I'm not reading or writing stories for children I like to crochet, play video games or watch animated films, and cuddle with my two cats.

Aisha Bushby

Why did you want to be an author?

I love making up stories; it's like playing a long game of pretend all day every day.

How did you get into writing?

I started by writing stories based on books I'd already read, and then I began inventing my own characters and worlds.

What is it like for you to write?

On the best days, writing is like jumping into a new world of my own imagination.

What is a book you remember loving reading when you were young?

I adored *The Animals of Farthing Wood* by Colin Dann. I really enjoyed following the stories of all the different animals, especially because I'd just moved to the UK so it was all very new to me.

Why this book?

I was inspired by *The Animals of Farthing Wood* to write from the point of view of different animals, but I also live in the countryside where I see (and hear!) lots of different animals.

Is there anything in this book that relates to your own experiences?

Bea the bat flies into someone's window and this happened to me! A bat flew into an open window while I was sleeping. I hid under the covers because it moved so quickly right above my head. Eventually, it flew back out of the window.

What do you hope readers will get out of the book?

I hope readers will pay more attention to the wild animals around them, because they're so wonderful and we're so lucky to be living with them!

Which of the animals in the book did you enjoy writing about most? Why?

I loved writing about Freddy the frog because I *love* frogs. They're one of my favourite animals (besides cats, and one of those also features in that story).

Do you have a top tip for something children could do to help wildlife near where they live?

I don't think children need to feel too responsible, as it's the grown-ups' jobs to look after wildlife. But if we avoid littering, and recycle what we can, this can help preserve their environment, keeping it safe and clean.

About the illustrator

A bit about me …

I'm an illustrator based in Brooklyn, New York! I've always loved painting and drawing, especially nature, fantasy creatures and fairy tales.

Gaby Verdooren

What made you want to become an illustrator?

Painting has always been my thing, and I always knew it was what I wanted to do when I grew up!

How did you get into illustration?

I did a summer illustration course at the Rhode Island School of Design. I was exposed to all kinds of illustration and all the ways I could apply what I was passionate about! I then went to college to study illustration.

What did you like best about illustrating this book?

Since I'm from the US, it was cool to learn about animals from a place I'm not familiar with! I love to do research, especially when it comes to animals and plants, so I was really happy to draw all the animals in this book.

Which was your favorite of the three animals to illustrate?

Definitely Bea, I love bats!

Is there anything in this book that is related to your own experiences?
I really love the natural world. It's one of the other things I'm passionate about besides art! This is a passion I share with my family. We name all the animals in our back-yard, and have feeders all over for them. We have binoculars by the kitchen window so we can see them from a safe distance, as well as as a back-yard camera!

How do you bring a character to life?
The characters sort of come to me as I draw, I don't go in with a plan most of the time. I let my pencil guide me and the ideas come as I go! I like to think the characters create themselves and I'm just the conduit to bring them to life.

Did you do research to help you with this book?
When you're an illustrator, you have to wear lots of different hats. You have to be an artist, a researcher, a writer, a designer, a whole team! A lot of research went into this book like all my other projects. And if you ask me, the research is my favourite part!

Do you prefer using photos to help you illustrate animals, or do you base your pictures on real life?
I rely a lot on photos from books or the internet for the work I do. I sometimes get the opportunity to use my own photos, but not that often. Maybe if I get to travel more in the future, I can get more of a photo folder going!

Book chat

Which of the animal stories in the book did you like best, and why?

Have you ever seen any of the animals in this book in real life?

If you could ask the author one question, what would it be?

What do you think humans can do to help look after animals like the ones in the book?

Which scene in this book stands out most for you? Why?

If you could be one of the animals in the book for a day, which would you choose? Why?

If you had to give the book a new title, what would you choose?

If you had to pick one scene to act out, which would you choose? Why?

Book challenge:
Think of something you could do to help animals during the winter.

Collins BIG CAT

Published by Collins
An imprint of HarperCollins*Publishers*

The News Building
1 London Bridge Street
London SE1 9GF
UK

Macken House
39/40 Mayor Street Upper
Dublin 1
D01 C9W8
Ireland

Text © Aisha Bushby 2023
Design and illustrations ©
HarperCollins*Publishers* Limited 2023

10 9 8 7 6 5

ISBN 978-0-00-862492-7

All rights reserved. No part of this publication may be reproduced, stored in a retrieval system, or transmitted in any form by any means, electronic, mechanical, photocopying, recording or otherwise, without the prior written permission of the Publisher or a licence permitting restricted copying in the United Kingdom issued by the Copyright Licensing Agency Ltd, 5th Floor, Shackleton House, 4 Battle Bridge Lane, London SE1 2HX.

British Library Cataloguing-in-Publication Data
A catalogue record for this publication is available from the British Library.

Download the teaching notes and word cards to accompany this book at:
http://littlewandle.org.uk/signupfluency/

Get the latest Collins Big Cat news at
collins.co.uk/collinsbigcat

Author: Aisha Bushby
Illustrator: Gaby Verdooren (Advocate Art)
Publisher: Lizzie Catford
Product manager and
    commissioning editor: Caroline Green
Series editor: Charlotte Raby
Development editor: Catherine Baker
Project manager: Emily Hooton
Content editor: Daniela Mora Chavarría
Copyeditor: Sally Byford
Proofreader: Gaynor Spry
Cover designer: Sarah Finan
Typesetter: 2Hoots Publishing Services Ltd
Production controller: Katharine Willard

Collins would like to thank the teachers and children at the following schools who took part in the trialling of Big Cat for Little Wandle Fluency: Burley And Woodhead Church of England Primary School; Chesterton Primary School; Lady Margaret Primary School; Little Sutton Primary School; Parsloes Primary School.

Printed and bound in the UK

MIX
Paper | Supporting responsible forestry
FSC™ C007454

This book contains FSC™ certified paper and other controlled sources to ensure responsible forest management.

For more information visit:
www.harpercollins.co.uk/green

Acknowledgements
The publishers gratefully acknowledge the permission granted to reproduce the copyright material in this book. Every effort has been made to trace copyright holders and to obtain their permission for the use of copyright material. The publishers will gladly receive any information enabling them to rectify any error or omission at the first opportunity.

p82 mauritius images GmbH /Alamy Stock Photo, p83t mauritius images GmbH/Alamy Stock Photo, p83b Nick Upton/Alamy Stock Photo, p84t Sergey Uryadnikov/Shutterstock, p84b Rudmer Zwerver/Alamy Stock Photo, p85 Ceri Breeze/Shutterstock.